Jingle Bear

Written by: Stephen Cosgrove
Illustrated by: Robin James

A Serendipity™ Book

PRICE STERN SLOAN
Los Angeles

D1497321

Dedicated to Laurie and Robby Plenge, may they find joy in Jingle Bear and the Season of Snow.

Stephen

Far beyond the newness of spring, and just a bit past the warmth of summer lies a land of wondrous delight. A place of golden leaves rustling in gentle breezes. A quiet place that seems to anticipate the changes to come. A place of preening goslings ready to fly south. A place of sparrows, hawks and robins, stopping here but not a part of here, resting on their difficult journey south. For this was Autumn-Fall, a place of yellow-golden delight in which to pause before the Season of Snow.

Of all the wondrous creatures that lived in the Autumn-Fall the bears were the most special. Just before the Season of Snow these animals hibernated and slept away the cold with dreams of spring and summer. But before they slept the bears had to eat, and eat they did! They raced about, scattering the golden aspen leaves, looking for a bit of this and a bit of that.

They ate tiny sweet nuts and plump ripe berries. The bears' favorite meal, though, was the golden honeycomb which was kept in the hollow oak tree. As bees buzzed about them, the bears sat covered in the sticky sweetness, eating more and more to protect them from the coming chill. They ate all this and much more, for the Season of Snow can be a long, cold winter.

All of the bears ate, that is, except for one little cub called Jingle Bear. Born earlier that spring of Big Poppa and Little Momma Bear, Jingle played and played instead of eating. The fuzzy bear knew he should eat but playing was just much more fun. Oh, sometimes he nibbled on a nut or two, but then he got distracted by a buzzing bee or a chattering chipmunk and off he went, looking for some new game to play.

Jingle's parents, Big Poppa and Little Momma Bear, tried to get him to eat the nuts and berries and honey of the forest but to no avail. Each time they sat down to a scrumptious meal of berries smothered in golden honey, Jingle Bear just wandered off — sometimes to catch a butterfly, sometimes to chase a bumbling bee up a tiny tree.

As he dashed off hither, thither and yon, Little Momma Bear shook her head and looked at Big Poppa, neither of them knowing what to do. They were very concerned, for they knew that Jingle had to eat all he could before the Season of Snow, the time of dreams and deep sleep.

Oh, how Jingle loved to play! But he also loved to listen to the chipmunks chatter and chatter, telling their wondrous tales of Father Snow. He sat and listened with rapt wonder as once again a chipmunk told the tale.

"Just after all the leaves have fallen from the trees, two days beyond the longest night, Father Snow comes crunching out of the north. His bag is full of gifts and goodies for all the creatures that stay awake during the long, cold winter. Gifts and presents galore, but the most special gift of all is the gift of Snow. Snow. White, crystalline snow which Father Snow spreads like a blanket over the forest. And with the snow comes a special silence, and the whole forest becomes a mighty, magic place."

Jingle Bear had heard this story a hundred times before, but each time he listened, spellbound, as he dreamed about Father Snow and the magic of his gift.

One day when Little Momma cornered Jingle Bear long enough to get him to eat some sweet hazel nuts, the little bear asked, "Momma, is there really a Father Snow?"

"Of course," Little Momma murmured as she fluffed up some pillows of thick green moss.

"Can I see him?" Jingle asked, crunching on a large, tasty nut.

"Of course not!" Little Momma said. "For when Father Snow arrives, you, like the rest of us, will be fast asleep."

But Jingle Bear did not reply. He quietly munched and munched, thinking of a marvelous plan.

Several weeks later when the days seemed shorter and the nights much colder, Big Poppa, Little Momma, and Jingle Bear prepared to go into their long winter's nap. They curled up together in a cave filled with juniper boughs and sweet-smelling sage and fell fast asleep.

Little Momma and Big Poppa snuggled up nose-to-nose, dreaming beautiful dreams of spring, but Jingle Bear just pretended to be asleep. First one eye opened and then another, and then the little furry bear set his plan in motion. Careful not to disturb his parents, he slipped out of the cave and out into the brisk fall day.

With an excited tingle, Jingle Bear dashed over a ridge and splashed through an icy stream. Over the rocks and through the naked willows and aspens of the valley he ran, looking for Father Snow.

But slowly he began to realize that there was no one else around and he snuffled and roared as loud as he could, "Father Snow! Father Snow! It's Jingle Bear! I'm here!" But the only sound was a stark echo ringing through the sleeping trees.

He ran and ran and finally came to a special hollow oak tree at the edge of a frozen meadow. "Hey, squirrels!" he yelled, "Father Snow is coming. Wake up! Wake up!"

Jingle shook and shook the tree until finally an old grizzled squirrel came out on the branch right above Jingle's head. "Of course Father Snow is coming," he grumbled, "and he'll come right after you go to bed! So, be off little bear and fall asleep, for Father Snow will only come in your dreams so deep." With that the old squirrel slipped back inside his warm old tree and fell back to blissful sleep.

"I guess I'm the only one who's going to see Father Snow and the magic gift," said Jingle Bear as he continued on his search for a waking dream.

He walked and walked, searching every-where for Father Snow, but he found nothing. Slowly, the bright sky began to darken with heavy black clouds, and though it was still daytime, Jingle found himself walking in the dark alone. Suddenly, one, then two crystal snowflakes gently floated down and landed at the very tip of his shiny black nose.

Jingle Bear looked around excitedly, for he knew that where there are snowflakes there must also be Father Snow and his gifts of the Season of Snow. But there was nothing around him save for the barren trees of the land of Autumn-Fall.

Sadly, Jingle Bear realized that Big Poppa and Little Momma Bear were right when they said that Father Snow wouldn't come until after he fell asleep. With heavy steps and frozen tears gliding down his furry face, the sad small bear turned to go back home.

"There probably isn't any old Father Snow anyway!" he muttered as he stumbled on his way.

He walked and walked, but with each step he took, he became more and more lost. To make matters worse, much worse, the snow was beginning to fall heavily now and he couldn't see where he was going at all. And Jingle Bear was getting colder and colder and feeling oh, so sleepy.

He was so sleepy, in fact, that he couldn't move another step. So, with his teeth chattering, Jingle Bear burrowed in at the base of a pine tree and fell into a dreamless sleep, muttering, "There is no Father Snow . . . There is no Father Snow!"

Poor Jingle Bear could have frozen right there and never thawed until spring — but wait! A shadowy shape with a long, flowing beard carefully picked him up and held him gently in his arms.

With a cheerful chuckle and a flash of magic, Father Snow whisked them both back to Jingle Bear's cave. Once there, he lay the peaceful sleeping bear right between Little Momma and Big Poppa.

"Yes," laughed the shadowy form, "there is a Father Snow. But I'll never come to you while you're awake because it is to sleep you must go." In a burst of starshine and moonglow he cast the land of Autumn-Fall into the magical Season of Snow. Then, with a sweep of his arm and a wave of his hand he gave Big Poppa, Little Momma and Jingle Bear the most precious gift of all, the gift of love — and then he disappeared.

A sleepy little bear opened one eye and wondered if all this magic was nothing more than a dream. Then, with a deep, deep sigh and one single yawn he fell into a warm winter's sleep.

THE HOLIDAYS ARE TOMORROW
YOUR HEART SEEMS TO LEAP
BUT TOMORROW WILL ONLY COME
RIGHT AFTER YOU FALL ASLEEP

Serendipity™ Books

Written by Stephen Cosgrove
Illustrated by Robin James

Enjoy all the delightful books in the Serendipity Series:

The above books, and many others, can be bought wherever books are sold, or may be ordered directly from the publisher.

PRICE STERN SLOAN

11150 Olympic Boulevard, 6th Floor, Los Angeles, California 90064